Dino

the
dingbat cat

By Jean Richardson

Illustrated by Nancy Garnett Peterson

EAKIN PRESS ᴇᴘ Austin, Texas

This book is dedicated with love
to my daughter Carol,
and Dino, her Dingbat Cat.

To Jori
Best Wishes!
Jean Richardson

REVISED EDITION
Copyright © 2000 and 1992
By Jean Richardson
Published in the United States of America
By Eakin Press
A Division of Sunbelt Media, Inc.
P.O. Drawer 90159 ◫ Austin, Texas 78709-0159
email: eakinpub@sig.net
🖥 website: www.eakinpress.com 🖥

ALL RIGHTS RESERVED.

Printed in Hong Kong

1 2 3 4 5 6 7 8 9

0-89015-869-X

Library of Congress Cataloging-in-Publication Data

Richardson, Jean.
    Dino, the dingbat cat / Jean Richardson : illustrated by Nancy Garnett Peterson.
        p.   cm.
    Summary: Although they love their mischievous cat, a family decides to send him away, untill he proves worth keeping.
    ISBN 0-89015-869-X
    [1. Cats—Fiction. 2. Stories in rhyme.] I. Peterson, Nancy Garnett, ill. II. Title
PZ8.3.R395Di   1992
[E]--dc20   92-17736
CIP
AC

Dino was a dingbat cat,

And everybody knew it.

Name anything cats shouldn't do,

Dino would surely do it.

Some days he was a savage lion,
A fierce, wild jungle kitty,
Attacking everything that dared
Invade his jungle city.

He'd hide behind the jungle plants,
And patiently he'd wait
'Till some unsuspecting victim
Came too close and met his fate.

Sometimes he'd be a 'fraidy cat
And not come out all day.
The smallest sound would scare him,
He'd be too afraid to play.

Dino loved a bubble bath—
He'd sit upon the tub
And slap the bubbles with his paws,
Then chase them 'cross the rug.

When the family ate their dinner
(If there was an empty chair),
Dino would sit and watch them,
Though he knew no one would share.

If the folks went off and left him
All alone at home,
He'd *yooowwwell* in his loudest voice
As through the house he'd roam.

He would crawl up in the window,
And impatiently would wait
To see the car returning
And the opening of the gate.

Then he'd slowly saunter over
As if he didn't care
That they'd been gone forever,
And left him lonesome there.

Dino had a person
Who was at his beck and call.
Whatever dingbat thing he did,
She loved him through it all.

When Dino dashed around the house
Attacking people's feet,
She'd laugh and call him "Silly Cat,"
And feed him kitty treats.

Though everybody else complained
And called him "Dingbat Cat,"
She gave him hugs and kisses,
Said she loved him. That was that!

When she went to bed at night
Between the sheets he'd creep,
Lay his head upon her pillow,
And pretend to be asleep.

But in the quiet after midnight
He'd start playing kitty games,
Breaking Mama's knick-knacks
and destroying precious things.

He would go to all the places
He was not supposed to go,
And they all would know he'd been there,
'Cause his kitty tracks would show.

So the family called a meeting.
Very sadly they decreed
The Dingbat Cat would have to go
To a home for "cats-in-need."

The girl was broken-hearted.
She really didn't know
How she could live without her cat,
Because she loved him so.

That night she held him tightly
As she cried herself to sleep,
While Dino licked her on the nose
and purred against her cheek.

In the wee hours of the morning
Dino rose to prowl about,
Padding softly to the kitchen
Hoping scraps had been left out.

While beneath the kitchen table
He received an awful fright.
Someone else was there before him,
Dressed in evil, hid by night.

In one hand he held a basket
He was loading up to take
All of Mama's precious knick-knacks
(The ones Dino didn't break).

At first Dino quaked in terror,
Then anger took its place,
And he leaped upon the burglar,
Scratching, clawing at his face.

Shocked, the burglar screamed in horror,
Threw his basket 'cross the floor.
Tried to pull the feline from him,
Tried to make it out the door.

And the family all was wakened
By the petrifying din.
They dialed 911 and pleaded,
"Come and help us, please come in!"

In the darkness in the kitchen,
Still the cat kept up his fight.
Draped across the burglar's shoulders,
Dino clawed with all his might.

Grabbing Dino by the tail,
The burglar slung him to the floor,
Dashed outside without the treasures,
Left poor Dino by the door.

Then the family called a meeting,
Right there in the dead of night,
Sitting 'round the kitchen table
All still shaking from the fright.

And they said they were mistaken
When they said he had to go,
And they hoped he would forgive them,
And they kissed and hugged him so!

Now when Dino goes a-dashing
And attacking people's feet,
They just laugh and call him "Silly Cat,"
And feed him kitty treats.